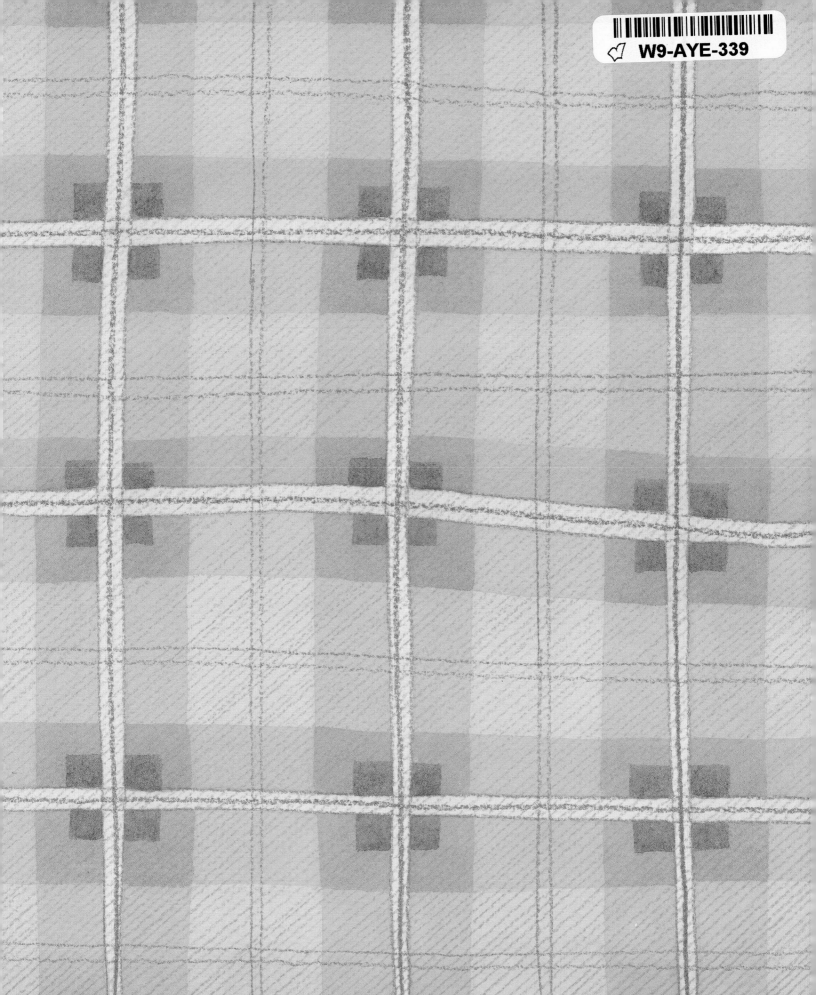

TRANSWORLD PUBLISHERS
61-63 Uxbridge Road, London W5 5SA
A division of The Random House Group Ltd

RANDOM HOUSE AUSTRALIA (PTY) LTD
20 Alfred St, Milsons Point, Sydney,
New South Wales 2061, Australia

RANDOM HOUSE NEW ZEALAND LTD
18 Poland Rd, Glenfield, Auckland 10, New Zealand

RANDOM HOUSE (PTY) LTD,
Endulini, 5a Jubilee Road, Parktown 2193, South Africa

Published in 2000 by Doubleday
a division of Transworld Publishers

Copyright © A.E.T. Browne and Partners 2000
Designed by Ian Butterworth

The right of Anthony Browne to be identified as the Author of
this work has been asserted in accordance with the Copyright,
Designs and Patents Act 1988

A catalogue record for this book is available
from the British Library

ISBN 0 385 600720

Printed in Italy

My Dad
Anthony Browne

D O U B L E D A Y

London New York Toronto Sydney Auckland

He's all right, my dad.

My dad isn't afraid of ANYTHING,

even the Big Bad Wolf.

He can jump right over the moon,

and walk on a tightrope (without falling off).

He could wrestle with giants,

or win the   fathers' race on
                              sports day, easily.

He's all right, my dad.

My dad can eat like a horse,

and he can swim like a fish.

He's as strong as a gorilla,

and as happy as a hippopotamus.

He's all right, my dad.

My dad's as big as a house,

and as soft as my teddy.

He's as wise as an owl,

and daft  as a brush.

He's all right, my dad.

My dad's a great dancer,

and a brilliant singer.

He's fantastic at football,

and he makes me laugh. A lot.

I love my dad.
And you know what?

HE LOVES ME!

(And he always will.)

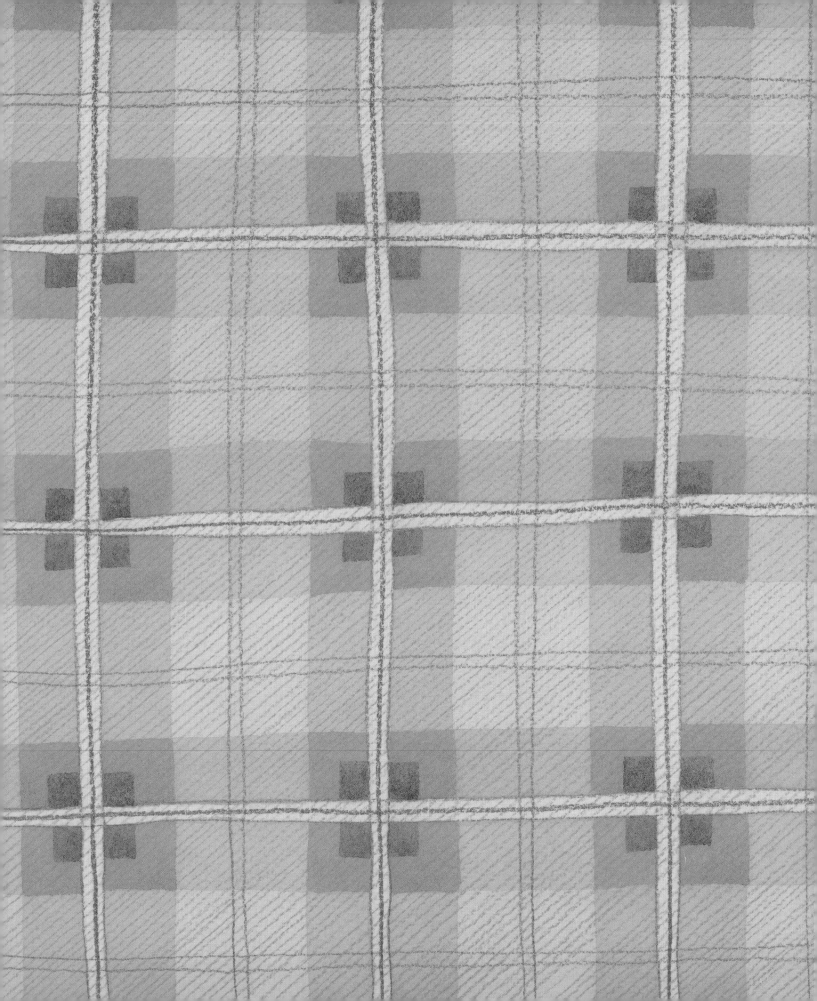